While I Am Little

While I Am Little

HEIDI GOENNEL

Tambourine Books

New York

To my father

While I am little I can
sleep with my Penguin
and wise old Teddy,

splash in big, muddy puddles
after it rains,

and be a cowboy all day long.

While I am little I can lick
all the icing in the bowl,

take Fluffie for a ride in my wagon,

and collect pennies and stamps
and lots of string.

While I am little I can help
Daddy build a treehouse
in our backyard,

ST. ANN'S SCHOOL
Salt Lake City, Utah

play with my best friend, Pete,

and read under the covers
way into the night.

While I am little I can make a snowman even taller than I am,

go fishing for the whole afternoon,

and see *The Blue-Toed Monster*
three times in a row.

And while I am little
I can keep growing up.

All rights reserved. No part of this book may be reproduced or
utilized in any form or by any means, electronic or mechanical,
including photocopying, recording, or by any information storage
or retrieval system, without permission in writing from the
Publisher. Inquiries should be addressed to Tambourine Books,
a division of William Morrow & Company, Inc.,
1350 Avenue of the Americas, New York, New York 10019.
Printed in the United States of America.
The full-color illustrations were painted in acrylic on canvas.

Library of Congress Cataloging in Publication Data

Goennel, Heidi. While I am little/by Heidi Goennel.—1st ed. p. cm.
Summary: A child describes splashing in puddles, collecting
things, reading under the covers, building snowmen, and other good
things about being young. [1. Growth —Fiction.] I. Title.
PZ7.G554Wi 1993 [E]—dc20 92-36795 CIP AC
ISBN 0-688-12371-6. —ISBN 0-688-12372-4 (lib. bdg.)
1 3 5 7 9 10 8 6 4 2
First edition